BOOK 1:
THE DISAPPEARING ACT

TEENY HOUDINI

BOOK 1:
THE DISAPPEARING ACT

BY **KATRINA MOORE**   ILLUSTRATIONS BY **ZOE SI**

KATHERINE TEGEN BOOKS
An Imprint of HarperCollins Publishers

Katherine Tegen Books is an imprint of HarperCollins Publishers.

Teeny Houdini #1: The Disappearing Act
Text copyright © 2022 by Katrina Moore
Illustrations copyright © 2022 by Zoe Si
All rights reserved. Printed in the United States of America.
No part of this book may be used or reproduced in any manner whatsoever without
written permission except in the case of brief quotations embodied in critical articles
and reviews. For information address HarperCollins Children's Books, a division of
HarperCollins Publishers, 195 Broadway, New York, NY 10007.
www.harpercollinschildrens.com

Library of Congress Control Number: 2021005541
ISBN 978-0-06-300461-0 (trade bdg.) — ISBN 978-0-06-300462-7 (pbk.)

Typography by Andrea Vandergrift
21 22 23 24 25   PC/LSCC   10 9 8 7 6 5 4 3 2 1
❖
First Edition

For my grandma,
who was full of magic!
—K.M.

To Kevin,
for bringing out the best
and funniest in me
—Z.S.

1

The Announcement

*D*ing. *Ding.* Ms. Stoltz rings the teacher's bell.

"I have an important announcement to share with you all," says Ms. Stoltz. She is my first-grade teacher. But I do not hear the important announcement. I am in the middle of a super-duper important project.

My name is Bessie Lee. And I don't want anyone to forget it. I write "Bessie Lee" *extra big* on my paper in swirly letters. Swirly letters make everything more special. That's what my sister, Bailey, says. She's a fifth grader. Fifth graders know everything.

I add stars to my name tag. My name looks so fancy!

"Ahem, Bessie . . . ," says Ms. Stoltz.

She stands in front of me.

"Yes, Ms. Stoltz?" I ask. I smile big so she knows I am happy to see her.

"Are you coloring on your homework?"

"It's my new name tag for my desk, Ms. Stoltz! Isn't it special?!"

"Quite . . . ," says Ms. Stoltz. She smiles. Then she slides me a new homework page.

Ms. Stoltz likes that my desk is in the front. That way she can tap it whenever she wants to. She is tapping my desk right now. I tap her finger back and say, "Abracadabra-poof!"

Abracadabra is a magic word. It makes

magic happen. Just like the name of the *Abra-cadabra: Magic for Kids* book that Gramma

bought me. The book is full of magic tricks! But Gramma can't read English. She only knows Chinese. And Mom and Daddy and Bailey are too busy to read it to me. So I don't know the tricks. I just make my own magic. I like the magic word *abracadabra*. I add "poof" because it's fancy, like me.

After I say "abracadabra-poof," Ms. Stoltz's finger disappears behind her back like magic. But her lips go funny, like this:

I like my desk in the front because I am teeny. In my family, I am too teeny to play with Bailey and her friends. She always says so! I am too teeny to sit at the big table at family parties. That's where they talk about "big-kid stuff." (But I always sneaky-listen, anyway.) I am too teeny to ride the big rides at Disney World. I have to go on the baby rides while Mom watches me. But I am *not* a baby!

At school, I am too teeny to be the calendar

You MUST BE THIS TALL!

helper at morning meeting. I can't point to the numbers on the top row. I am too teeny to reach the big-kid swings at recess. All the other first graders can reach them.

Also, I am too teeny to sit in the back. If I sat in the back, then I would not be able to see over Brayden's big head. But I don't say that out loud because that's not nice. I like my desk in the front. I can reach Ms. Stoltz whenever I want to.

"Bessie, please pay attention. I'm in the middle of a very important announcement."

"Okay," I say. *Paying attention* means I have

to stop. And sit very still. And not blink. And make my ears very big, too.

I stop. I sit very still. But then I look at Margo. Margo sits next to me. She is wearing a very sparkly bow in her hair. It makes rainbow dots all over her desk. Ooh-la-laddie! *Ooh-la-laddie* means something makes my eyes go big! This is why I cannot sit still. Margo's bow is sparkly. It makes extra fancy rainbow dots on her desk!

I tap-tap-tap the rainbow dots. If I tap each one, abracadabra-poof! Maybe something magical will happen!

"Ms. Stoltz!" says Margo. "Bessie keeps touching my desk."

I take my finger back. I frown at Margo.

Margo always tattles on me for breaking the rules. Like "keep your hands to yourself."

And "always raise your hand to talk." When Margo raises her hand, she holds it high. And still. My hand is teeny. I have to wave it. Otherwise, Ms. Stoltz won't see it.

But Ms. Stoltz always calls on Margo. Margo always follows the rules. I know the rules. But sometimes I forget. And anyways, I would not tattle on Margo. *That's not nice.*

"Bessie . . . ," says Ms. Stoltz.

"Yes, Ms. Stoltz?" I say. I smile big.

"Hands to yourself," says Ms. Stoltz. Margo grins. I huff.

"Yes, Ms. Stoltz," I say. I look down. Now I am teenier.

"I am trying to tell you all about the talent show . . . ," says Ms. Stoltz.

"THE TALENT SHOW?!" I shout. I pop out of my seat. "WHY DIDN'T YOU *SAY* SO?"

I stop when I see the look on Ms. Stoltz's face. I stand very still. I do not blink. I make my ears very, very big.

Ms. Stoltz tells us that the First Grade Talent Show will be in one week!

She says, "In one week, you can perform your talent onstage. Your families will be invited. We will vote on who has the biggest talent. The winner of our talent show will perform at our "Courage to Be Zesty" school

assembly this month. All of Annalise Jean Memorial Elementary will be watching that assembly. What a big deal that will be!"

I think about what Ms. Stoltz says. Winning the talent show is a *big* deal. If I win the talent show, everyone will think I am *big*, too. I will not be too teeny to play with friends at recess. I will not be too teeny to go places with my family. I will be big, big, big.

Ooh-la-laddie! I jump up and down. "Hooray!" I cheer.

Now I just need to find a big talent to win the show!

2

Talent Trouble

On the bus, I bounce up and down in my seat. I can't wait to tell Gramma about the talent show. I look out the bus window. I see Gramma! Her hair is silver and black. It's curled tightly on top of her head. She is wearing a silk shirt. Just like she does every day. Today it is her lucky red shirt. It's buttoned all the way up. Gramma stays home all day. But she likes to be fancy, like me!

Lurch. The bus slows to a stop. I hear

Gramma laughing with Ms. Alrahhal. Ms. Alrahhal is a nice old lady. She lives down the street. Gramma only speaks Chinese and Ms. Alrahhal only speaks Arabic. Sometimes, they do not know what the other is saying. But they are still very good friends.

I jump through the doors superfast.

"Bessie . . . ," says Ms. Pat, our bus driver. She sounds very tired today. "Please don't run."

"Okay, Ms. Pat. Goodbye!" I say. I smile really big. I show all my teeth and gums, so she knows I am using my good manners. Just like Mom told me to do. Then I run to Gramma.

"Gramma! I'm going to be in the talent show!"

"*Mut yeh?*" asks Gramma. That means "what" in Chinese.

I want to tell Gramma about the talent show in Chinese. But I do not know the right Chinese words. So I try to use my hands and show her what I want to say. That's how we talk to each other. Gramma talks in Chinese. And I act out what I want to say. Like a stage performer!

I do not know what to do with my hands so I flap them like a bird.

And then I twirl.

And then I skip.

And then I run around Gramma and Ms. Alrahhal in circles like our class pet hamster, Rufus.

And then I realize that I do not really know what my talent is in Chinese *or* in English. I plop down onto the sidewalk. I look up and make a funny face at Gramma.

She giggles. Then covers her mouth. And shakes her head. She always does that. She thinks I'm silly.

"Gah Yee!" says Gramma. *Gah Yee* is my Chinese name.

Gramma always calls me by my Chinese name when I sit down in places that are not my bed.

"Sit with me, Gramma," I say. I pat the hard sidewalk.

Gramma shakes her head. But she kneels down in front of me. She cups my cheeks with her hands. And gives a little squeeze. That always makes us both giggle.

My sister, Bailey, pops out from inside our house.

"Bessie, you better get up before Mom and Dad get home," Bailey shouts from across the lawn. She leaves the door open for us.

She is right. I pop up. Then I help Gramma stand up. I zoom into the house because I have something very important to do.

I am going to find a talent for the talent show! I run right to my room. My pet rabbit, Baby Rabbit, has been waiting for me all day.

"Hi, Baby Rabbit!" I say.

I give her a big hug and squeeze tight.

Baby Rabbit and I eat snacks that I've hidden under my bed. I have lots to choose from.

I can have a candy bar that I sneaky-snuck from Bailey's trick-or-treat bag last year. Or I can have my *dan tat.* That's an egg custard mini pie Gramma makes us. Only as a special dessert sometimes. It's my favorite! I put an extra one in my pocket last week. Then I saved it under my bed.

"Do you want my mini pie, Baby Rabbit?"

She just looks at me. Maybe it is yucky now. *Boo.* I throw it away.

I grab a bag of cheesy doodles instead. I have a million gazillion bags of cheesy doodles under my bed. For emergencies. *Emergencies* are when I really, really want something. And Mom and Daddy say no. And Gramma fell asleep watching too many Chinese soap shows. So she cannot help me either.

Focus! Focus! I put on my thinking cap that Mom bought me from the store that time when I was a good girl. *Good* means I stopped pouting. And stomping my foot. And rolling on the floor.

I tap-tap-tap my head. And I say, "Abracadabra-poof," my extra fancy magic word that makes magic appear. Maybe it will make some magic ideas appear into my mind.

I make a list of things I like to do. Maybe this will help me find my talent.

THINGS i LIKE to do:
- cut and style Bailey's Barbies' hair.
- play with Baby Rabbit.
- put crayons into Gramma's soup so it turns rainbow colors.

Finding a talent is hard work. I eat another bag of cheesy doodles.

Then Baby Rabbit and I zoom down the

hallway to Bailey's room. It is locked. But I hear her music inside. Baby Rabbit sniffs the door.

"HELLO!" I yell. "YOUR DOOR IS LOCKED!"

"I know!" says Bailey through the door.

She does not unlock the door. I jiggle it and jiggle it and jiggle it once more. This way she knows that I am still there. I shout, "HELLO! HELLO! HELLO! HELLO! HELLO!" until she opens the door.

"Jeez, Bessie," says Bailey. Bailey shakes her head. She huffs really loud. This is what she does when she is upset with me. She does it a lot. Huffing loudly looks fun. I try it, too.

Bailey turns her back on me. Then she puts the music back on. She does not pay attention to me. But I have an important question.

"What's my talent?"

"Being annoying!" she says.

"Is that a talent?"

"SKEDADDLE!" Bailey shouts. "I'M BUSY!"

"What is *skedaddle?*" I ask.

"It means leave!" says Bailey.

But I do not leave.

The Great Houdini!

I am still in my sister's room. Even though she told me to leave.

"I need your help," I say to Bailey. I use my superserious voice.

Her arms are crossed. She crosses them when she does not like what I do. She does this a lot! Like when she says "leave" and I do not leave her room.

"Will you please help?" I ask.

I smile big. I blink my eyes real slow. This way she knows I am trying to be sweet. I whisper to Baby Rabbit. She flops her ears down. She twitches her nose. This is her sweet face, too.

"Oh, all right," says Bailey. She sighs. She taps my hat. Then she pets Baby Rabbit between her ears.

"What's up, Houdini?"

"Who-dee-nee," I repeat. "Who's Houdini?"

"Harry Houdini? He's the greatest magician of all time. That's who you look like right now," says Bailey. She taps my hat again.

"The greatest magician? Of. All. Time?" I ask.

I am trying not to yell. Yelling scares Baby Rabbit. But I am too excited! So instead I bounce, bounce, bounce.

"I want to know more!" I say.

"Look," says Bailey. She opens her laptop. It has DANCE IS LIFE stickers all over it. She types some big words into Google Search. She clicks.

"Oh. Wow. He has his own website," says Bailey. She scrolls and clicks. Scrolls and clicks. I scoot closer to her. I pull her purple

blanket on top of my lap. It has fancy, magical stars all over it. I trace them with my finger.

Bailey reads silently and moves her lips. But it's too fast for me to read her lips.

"Hey, look at this," says Bailey. "His wife's name was Bess, like you."

"Bess like Bessie!" I say.

"Yeah," says Bailey. She chuckles.

Bailey clicks on another website.

"Here's another article," says Bailey.

"'The Greatest Magicians of All Time,'" says Bailey. She reads out loud to me. "'Harry Houdini was the greatest escape artist of all time,'" she says. Then she turns her back to me. I think she is done helping me. She goes back to dancing.

"What's an escape artist?" I ask.

Bailey turns around again. She huffs.

I huff, too. Bailey rolls her eyes.

"An escape artist is someone who disappears," says Bailey.

"Disappears? That's a talent?"

"And it's magic, too?!" I ask.

I am bouncing so fast that Baby Rabbit tucks into my elbow. I stop bouncing. I pat her little head.

"Sorry, Baby Rabbit," I whisper.

"Yes, Bessie. Magic is a talent. Disappearing is a talent. It's perfect for you!" says Bailey. She walks over and pats Baby Rabbit, too.

"Now scram!" says Bailey.

She shuts her laptop.

Scram means go away very fast, like a disappearing magician.

Just like Houdini.

Just. Like. Me.

I disappear back into my room and plop onto my bed. From under my pillow, I pull out the *Abracadabra: Magic for Kids* book that Gramma bought me. I pet the picture of the rabbit on the front page. It looks just like Baby Rabbit. Bailey said Houdini's wife was someone named Bess. Bess is like Bessie.

Just like me.

I open up my notebook. Baby Rabbit snuggles under my leg. I write one more thing I like to do.

I will do magic for the talent show. And be the greatest magician of all time. Just like Houdini.

I need to make something disappear. That will make me win! Then no one is going to think I am teeny. Because winning the talent show is a big, big, big deal.

"Time to plan the show, Baby Rabbit!"

4

The Disappearing Dinner

The first part of planning a show is setting up a big stage! But I do not have a stage. So I need to make one. I will use my bed!

Baby Rabbit helps me. We grab my pillows. We grab Mom and Daddy's pillows. We grab Bailey's pillows, too. I do not grab Gramma's pillows. They smell like mothballs. I throw all the pillows onto my bed. This will make it bigger. But it still does not look big enough to be a stage.

Ta-da!

Ta-da is what I say when I make a big surprise.

I am not so teeny anymore!

"Look how tall I am," I say to my audience. An audience is the people who watch you onstage.

My audience is Baby Rabbit.

Also, Dragon, Tiger, Pink Kitty, Ana, Elsa, Brown Bear, Blue Bear, and Boo-Boo Bear.

Now what?

I hop off my stage. I pick up my *Abracadabra: Magic for Kids* book. The magician on the front has a cape. That's it! The next part of planning the show is looking like a magician.

I need a magic cape!

But what's that yummy smell? It smells like something sweet. And steamy. And salty. Like Gramma's mini spareribs.

"*GAH YEE!*" Gramma yells my Chinese name from downstairs. It must be dinnertime. Gramma likes everyone to come to dinner super-duper fast. I will go down in *just one minute*.

First, I need a fancy magic cape. With streamers. And sparkly stickers. And ribbons.

I open the hallway closet. I see the box I want. Baby Rabbit jumps to the top shelf. She sniffs the box.

"Are they in there, Baby Rabbit?!"

She gives me two ears up. Good thing I am a good climber. But too bad that I am too teeny to catch the box. It falls down. *BOOM!*

Ooh-la-laddie! My eyes go big. This is extra fancy! There are streamers. And sparkly stickers. And ribbons. All over me. I am covered in them! Wait until my family sees me!

I zoom downstairs super-duper fast. Everyone is already sitting at their dinner table seats.

"Mom! Daddy!" I give Mom a hug first.

Mom's hair is wet. It's dripping on her soft Mickey Mouse T-shirt.

Daddy always jokes that this is Mom's uniform. A uniform is something you wear all the time.

Mom is a pharmacist. A pharmacist gives you medicine when you're sick. Mom is a pharmacist at the hospital. She is around germs all day. So she likes to shower as soon as she comes home. Then she wears her Mickey Mouse T-shirt. And her favorite jeans. She's had those for forever!

"I like your uniform, Mom," I say. I wink at Daddy.

"Yeah, yeah," says Mom jokingly. She smiles.

Daddy giggles. He likes when I joke, too.

Daddy is still wearing his work clothes. Today he is wearing a fancy tie. He only wears a tie when he goes to court. Daddy is a lawyer at a place in Washington, DC, with lots of letters in its name. Every day he takes the train from Washington, DC, and then Mom picks him up. Mom and Daddy drive home together from work. They go everywhere together. Even when it's just to the post office.

Mom always likes the family to do things together. Like eat family dinner together every day.

I hug Daddy. His face is prickly. He smells like coffee. Daddy says coffee is for all the time, not just the morning.

"Hi, sweetie," says Daddy. He hugs me like a bear.

"Sit down, please," says Mom. "We've been waiting for you."

"Nice outfit . . . ," says Bailey. She is staring at the streamers. And ribbons. I wrapped them around my shoulders. And the sparkly stickers. I stuck them all over my shirt. And face.

"Thank you!" I say. And then everybody laughs. I am so funny.

Mom fills my bowl of white rice with stinky bitter melon.

I try to stop her. "No more!"

"It's good for you, Bessie," she says. Mom always says that. But bitter melon is bitter. I do *not* like it. I do like Gramma's mini spareribs, though!

"Mini spareribs, please!" Gramma only gives me two.

Mom is not looking. I grab the

tongs and take ten more. I gobble them up. All that is left in my bowl is the stinky bitter melon. And too much rice. Everyone talks at the same time. No one is paying attention to me.

I will practice my first magic trick: the disappearing dinner!

I sneaky-slide under the table with my bowl. I squish my rice and stinky bitter melon into Daddy's slipper. I sit back on my chair superfast.

Ta-da!

I made a big surprise. My bowl is empty. My first disappearing trick!

I tip my hat and bow my head. No one is paying attention to me.

"May I be excused, please? I am all done," I

ask. I tug-tug-tug Mom's sleeve until she pays attention to me.

"Let me see your bowl," she says.

"All done," I say.

"How about your homework?" she asks.

"All done," I say. But my face turns red. I did not do it yet. Because I am in the middle of a super-duper important project. I need to finish planning the show. Then I will do my homework.

I have to make my extra fancy magic cape.

I zoom away.

I know just the thing!

5

A Magic Lesson

I am done making my magic cape! It is extra fancy. I cannot wait to show it off at school tomorrow! But I have to keep it a secret. I used Bailey's blanket to make it. It is soft. And puffy. And purple. And full of magical stars. I tuck it under my bed. This way no one will see.

"BESSIE!" Daddy calls from downstairs.

Uh-oh. He found his slipper.

"GET DOWN HERE, BESSIE!" shouts Daddy.

"Okay, Daddy," I say. But I do not zoom downstairs. I do not want to see Daddy upset. I walk very slowly. My body is very heavy now, like an elephant. I tiptoe down the stairs.

"Hi, Daddy," I say. My head is down.

"Bessie," says Daddy. "Did you do this?" he asks. He holds his slipper full of rice. It stinks like bitter melon.

I slowly nod. I sniffle. I did not mean to make Daddy's slipper smell like bitter melon.

I start to cry.

"Bessie," says Daddy softly, "this was not nice. Gramma worked hard to cook you dinner. You threw it away in my slipper. Also, you lied to Mom. You said you finished dinner. But you did not. You need to think before you act. Okay?"

"Okay, Daddy," I say.

Daddy makes me clean his slipper. Then he makes me eat two pieces of bitter melon. *Yuck.* "Mom says it's good for you," he says. "It will help you grow."

Because I'm teeny, I think. I will not have to eat bitter melon when I am big.

"Did you learn your lesson?" asks Daddy.

"Yes, Daddy," I say.

"Good," he says. He ruffles my hair.

I go back to my room soon after. I lock my door. I am still sad. Daddy's slipper is fixed.

But my magic trick was ruined!

I pull out my notebook. I write the lesson I learned.

DO NOT LET ANY1
FIND WHAT U ~~DISPIRD~~
DISAPPEARED

Like rice in your daddy's slipper. Now I learned my lesson!

Knock. Knock.

"Bessie," says Mom through the door. "Open the door."

I open the door.

"Hi, Mom," I say. I stand tall. I put my hands by my sides. I look her in the eyes so she knows I have good manners.

"What is this mess in the hallway?!" she asks. She points to the closet.

Oh yeah. I remember. The streamers. And ribbons. And sparkly stickers. The fallen-down box in the hallway. The box I was too teeny to reach.

"Sorry," I say. "I'll clean it."

"Right now," says Mom.

"Okay," I say.

I clean. And clean. And clean.

Everyone else is downstairs playing cards together. And laughing.

But not me. I am still cleaning.

Mom comes back upstairs. She reminds me to clean. Because sometimes I forget. And I start to play with the streamers.

I clean. And clean. And clean. For a million gazillion hours.

I think about the lesson I learned. *Do not let anyone find what you disappeared.*

"Do not let anyone find what you disappeared. Do not let anyone find what you disappeared." I say it again and again. I do not want to forget this lesson.

Harry Houdini was the greatest magician of all time.

So I will be like Houdini.

And I will perform the greatest disappearing act.

Then I will win the talent show.

That will make me a big deal!

Then I won't be too teeny to play with my family.

The next morning, I pop out of bed. I cannot wait to show off my magic cape. My secret magic cape.

I put on my puffy winter coat before I go downstairs. I do not want Bailey to see my cape. The cape I used her blanket to make. I had to! It is soft. And puffy. And purple.

I come down for breakfast.

Bailey says, "Why are you wearing your coat? Winter's more than two months away. It's seventy degrees outside."

"I'm cold," I say.

I do not tell her that I cut up her blankie. That's how I made my magical cape. That would make her mad. It is not nice to make people mad.

"Then why are you sweating?" she says. She hands me a toasted Pop-Tart.

"Just 'cause," I say.

She does not ask me any more questions. We eat our Pop-Tarts without talking and wait for the school bus to arrive.

Almost time to show off my magic cape!

6

The Disappearing Hamster

When I get to school, I race to the carpet.

I am so hot. But I do not take off my puffy coat. I am hiding my magic cape underneath. I am going to share it at morning meeting. I am so excited!

Ms. Stoltz rings the bell and says, "Find a circle spot for morning meeting."

I am already sitting at the carpet. I am already raising my hand. When she calls on

me, I will share my secret. I will show off my magic cape.

"Good morning, class," says Ms. Stoltz.

"Good morning, Ms. Stoltz," everyone says.

She does not pay attention to me. I stand up and wave.

"Bessie . . . please sit down and wait for sharing time," says Ms. Stoltz.

Waiting is the worst.

We all greet each other in Sanskrit this week. *Namaste* is how you say hello.

"Namaste, Chris."

"Namaste, Ella."

"Namaste, Margo."

"Namaste, Gorkem."

"Namaste, Bessie."

When it's finally my turn, I open my mouth to share my magic news. But Ms. Stoltz makes her lips go all funny in a straight line again.

So I say, "*Na-ma-ste*, Brayden."

I wait. And wait. And wait until it is time to share.

Ms. Stoltz finally says, "Who has something to share today? Bessie?"

"WOW!" says Chris.

"That's so cool!" says Ella.

"I want one!" says Gorkem.

"Me too!" says Brayden.

"You're *not* magic," says Margo. "Magicians are grown-ups. Like the one that was at my birthday party. You're just a teeny kid."

I was not invited to Margo's birthday party.

"I *am* magic!" I say.

"What magic can you do?" asks Margo. She puts her hands on her hips.

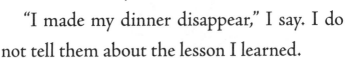

"Umm . . . ," I say. My voice shakes. I don't know what to say.

"I made my dinner disappear," I say. I do not tell them about the lesson I learned.

"I think you're lying," says Margo.

"I will make something disappear today, too," I say. I put my hands on my hips. Margo rolls her eyes. She does not believe me.

Ms. Stoltz rings her bell.

"I will prove it," I whisper to Margo.

We go back to our desks. Ms. Stoltz is choosing new classroom helpers.

I imagine all the different things I can make disappear in class. I remember my lesson: *Do not let anyone find what you disappeared.*

What could I make disappear? All the Hula-Hoops? But then Ella couldn't use them at recess. Margo's lunch? But then she'd be hungry. Margo's homework? But then she'd get in trouble. I don't want her to get in trouble. Even if she tattles on me all the time.

I snap out of it when I hear Ms. Stoltz ask, "Who would like to clean out Rufus's cage today?"

"I WILL! I WILL!" I shout. I raise my hand.

"Thank you, Bessie," says Ms. Stoltz.

"Thank *you*, Ms. Stoltz," I say. I sneaky-smile.

I rip a page out of my writing journal. I write a note. I use special markers.

DEAR CLASS,
I WILL MAKE RUFUS
DISAPPEAR. I WILL
DO THIS WITH MAGIC.
~~SINSEERLEY~~ FROM,
BESSIE

Ms. Stoltz turns around. I pass the note to Ella.

"Wow!" she whispers. Then she passes the note to Brayden.

It is snack and chat time. Our whole class surrounds me. Ms. Stoltz is talking to another teacher.

It is time for my second disappearing act: the disappearing hamster!

"Show us, Bessie! Show us!" says Ella.

"There's no way you're going to do it," says Margo.

I feel teeny. And a teensy bit nervous. Everybody is paying attention to me.

"For this trick, I will make Rufus vanish into thin air!" I say.

"No way," says Margo. I do not pay attention to her.

But I do not know how I will make Rufus disappear. I sweat.

I hold the sides of my cape with my hands. I wiggle my arms around to warm up. I am still holding the cape. But my right hand is stuck. It will not wiggle.

I yank my cape harder.

Everyone watches me. I yank my cape harder. It is still stuck.

They all stare. They watch me yank the cape. It is stuck on the cage. But they do not know that. They think I know what I'm doing.

But I do not know what to do. Maybe I will say the extra fancy magic word. Then, maybe, Rufus will magically disappear! For real!

Yank! Finally, my hand is unstuck.

I cover Rufus's cage with my cape.

I say, "One, two, three, abracadabra-poof!"
I open up my cape. Glitter flies out from my
cape pocket. That's my secret pocket. I stapled
it on to the cape!

When the glitter settles, all that is left is an
empty hamster cage. Rufus has disappeared.

"WOW!!!" says Chris.

"That's so cool!" says Ella.

"Can I be your friend?" asks Gorkem.

"Me too!" says Brayden.

"Why is his cage open?" asks Margo.

But no one is paying attention to her.

Because I did magic. Just like Houdini.

7

Where Is Rufus?

Ooh-la-laddie. My eyes get real big. I *am* magic. I just made the class pet hamster, Rufus, disappear.

Except . . .

What happened to Rufus?

"Where is Rufus?" Ms. Stoltz asks the class.

I sweat.

I do not know. And I do not know how to bring him back.

Margo raises her hand to tattle on me. But—

Brrring!

I am saved by the recess bell. Everyone lines up superfast. They all walk out to recess.

But I do not walk out with the class. I need to find Rufus. Where is he?!

I crawl under the desk near his cage. Maybe Rufus is under here.

He is not.

I lie on the ground so I am teenier. Like a hamster. My eyes zoom all around the room. Maybe I will see him hiding.

I do not.

"Bessie, what are you doing?" asks Ms. Stoltz.

"Oh, nothing . . . ," I say. I get up off the floor.

I do not tell Ms. Stoltz that I am looking for Rufus. Because then she will know that I made him disappear. And then she will be mad at me. I do not want Ms. Stoltz to be mad at me. I want Rufus to be okay.

"Let's go to recess," says Ms. Stoltz.

She holds the door open for me.

"Okay," I say. I walk outside with my head down.

Outside at recess, I find a spot to sit and think. I tap-tap-tap my head with my finger. I am trying to get a good idea into my head.

How can I bring Rufus back?!

I do not know.

Is he okay?

I do not know.

Will he come back?

I. Do. Not. Know.

I am hot. And cold. And my heart beats fast, like *bum-bum-bum-bum*. I can hear it. It is so loud.

I am worried about Rufus.

I walk in small circles to think. How can I bring Rufus back? I do not even know how I did the trick! This is an important lesson. I tap-tap-tap my brain so I remember. I say to myself, "Always know how you did the trick!"

I wish Rufus were back.

That's it!

Maybe I can make a wish. I can find a twinkling star. And make a wish on it. I will wish that Rufus comes back.

I look up. I search the sky. It is hard to see stars when the sky is sunny.

"Bessie!" Ella runs over to me. "Want to play?" she asks me.

"You want to play *with me*?!" I ask. No one ever asks me to play.

"Yeah!" says Ella. "We can swing!"

"Oh," I say. I think about the time I tried to sit on the swing earlier this year. But it was too high. I jumped. My butt plopped on the ground instead of the swing. And Margo saw. And laughed. "I'm too teeny to go on the swings."

"Really?" says Ella.

I bet she will walk away now. But she doesn't!

"Well, we can Hula-Hoop!" Ella says.

"Okay!" I say. But I still need to find Rufus. So I will only Hula-Hoop for a minute.

Margo is Hula-Hooping, too. So I bring my Hula-Hoop to the other side of Ella so I am not near her.

Ella is a super-duper Hula-Hooper.

"Are you going to Hula-Hoop for the talent show?" I ask.

I try to copy her by swinging my hips around. But my Hula-Hoop is too big for my teeny hips.

"Yeah!" Ella says. "I can do two or three at one time."

"Cool!" I say.

"Not as cool as magic," says Ella.

"Can you even do magic?" asks Margo. She

walks over and is right next to me now. "I still don't think you did it. And I don't think you can do it again." She sways with the Hula-Hoop. Her sparkly bow keeps shining like stage lights.

"Just wait and see," I say.

"Wait and see!" says Ella.

"Yeah!" say Brayden, Gorkem, and Chris all together.

Margo just rolls her eyes.

"Where is Rufus, for real?" asks Margo. She looks right at me.

"I can't tell you. It's magic!" I say.

I smile. And stick my chin up. Now I am a teeny bit taller. But really, I am worried to death about Rufus! I do not know where Rufus is.

But now I know what *worried to death* means. Mom says it to me when I run and hide under the clothes racks when we are at the mall. And when she calls my name and I don't answer for a long time because I am pretending to be a frozen statue. And when I play ninja and climb onto the top shelf of the kitchen pantry. I always make Mom worry to death.

Now Rufus has disappeared. Because of me. I do not know how to bring him back. I cannot pretend to smile anymore.

I need to find Rufus. I need to make sure he is okay. Otherwise I will for sure die from all this worrying.

I need a magic trick to make Rufus come back.

R I P
BESSIE LEE
~Died from
worrying about
Rufus

8

Not Magic

After recess, I remember about the talent show. But I am still thinking about Rufus, too. So I will make Rufus reappear at the talent show. *Reappear* means "come back." Like when you disappear by magic. And then you are here again. But *how?*

Idea 1:

HUMAN
HAMSTER TREAT
TRICK

PEANUT
BUTTER

Idea 2:

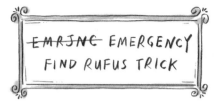

~~EMRJNC~~ EMERGENCY
FIND RUFUS TRICK

THE DAILY CHRONICLE

LOST RUFUS!

—LIKES PEANUT BUTTER—
REWARD:
ONE MAGIC TRICK!

"Bessie . . . ," says Ms. Stoltz. She stands by the door. She tap-tap-taps her clipboard.

"Can you line up for our nature walk? Bring your writing journal, please. We will write down our observations."

Ooh-la-laddie! My eyes get big. "WHY DIDN'T YOU SAY SO?!" I yell.

I love nature walks.

I get in line behind Ella. She saved me a spot.

When we get outside, we walk around the

schoolyard. Ms. Stoltz has us stop to write in our journals. I do not remember what I am supposed to write. So I write a list and draw pictures of the magic tricks I performed.

MAGIC TRICKS SO FAR:
#1 dinner disappears
#2 Rufus disappears
?? ??
TO DO:
#3 Make Rufus COME BACK!
#4 Make Margo disappear?

Next, we walk past the school vegetable garden. Margo runs over to the cabbage patch.

"LOOK! LOOK!" shouts Margo.

She does not raise her hand. But I do not tattle on her. She points toward the cabbage.

"Walk, please," says Ms. Stoltz.

Everyone runs over.

"IT'S RUFUS!!" screams Margo. "He did not disappear. I told you! He *just* escaped! *Bessie* let him out of his cage."

Everyone gasps. Even me.

"You are *not* magic, Bessie," says Margo. She flips her hair. Her sparkly bow shines on me. Just like a spotlight. "You're not a great magician. You're just a teeny kid."

Margo picks up Rufus and hands him to Ms. Stoltz.

I do not know what to say. I cross my arms. I hug my writing journal real tight. My eyes fill with tears. But I do not blink. Because I do not want Margo to see me cry. Then she will think I am a baby. Just a teeny, weeny baby.

"Oh my," says Ms. Stoltz. "Everyone, I think it's time to go back inside." She pats me lightly on the shoulder. That makes the tears fall down my cheeks.

"We'll talk inside, Bessie."

Everyone walks back to the classroom in a line. Even though I am farther behind, I can still hear them talking.

"She's *not* magic!" says Chris.

"She faked it," says Gorkem.

"I know!" says Brayden.

"*I told you,*" says Margo.

Only Ella turns around to look for me. But I turn my head away.

I pretend I am not paying attention to what everyone is saying.

After school, I get off the bus. I do not say one word. Gramma talks to Ms. Alrahhal outside our house. She does not pay attention to me.

When we walk in the house, I smell Gramma's pork and papaya soup. Bailey sits at the kitchen counter. She is eating Gramma's soup and reading a big book.

I climb onto the stool next to her. She doesn't look up at me.

Gramma scoops soup from the pot into a

bowl. She put extra papaya pieces in it because she knows I love papaya. She slides it in front of me. I do not pick up my spoon.

"What's wrong with you?" asks Bailey.

"Nothing," I say. Bailey rolls her eyes.

I am not hungry for soup. I do not even try to put crayons in the bowl. Even though I love to make rainbow soup.

I pull my magic cape out of my backpack. I hug it close.

"BESSIE!" Bailey shouts. "Is that *my* blanket? My favorite blanket?!" Bailey turns tomato red.

Uh-oh.

She yanks it from my arms. "BESSIE!!"

I open my mouth to say sorry. But I cannot make words. There is a big, invisible rock stuck in my throat. *Invisible* means you can't see it. But it is there for real. Because the words I want to say cannot come out. *I am sorry. I stole Bailey's favorite blanket. And I ruined it. She is mad. She is sad. Because of me. I am sorry.*

The invisible rock blocks my words. I say nothing.

Then . . . I just cry. I fall to the floor. I crawl into a teeny ball. I cry. And cry. And cry. I cannot stop.

"*Ay yah!*" cries Gramma. *Ay yah* is what she says when she is worried. Gramma hurries over to me. She holds me in her lap.

"You're acting ridiculous," says Bailey. "And you're not even magic."

"Yes I am," I whimper. But I am not sure if this is true. Gramma rubs my back. "What about the dinner I made disappear?" I feel a little bit mightier when I remember that.

Bailey rolls her eyes. She chucks my magic cape onto the floor.

"You hid it in Dad's slipper! It's not magic if we know the trick," says Bailey. "Ugh!" she groans. Then she stomps out of the kitchen.

Finally, I am done crying. But inside I am still sad.

Gramma carries me off the floor. She sits me on the stool in the kitchen. Gramma gently lifts my chin. She tries to feed me soup.

"No, thank you," I whisper. Gramma doesn't listen. She brings the spoon closer to my mouth. I shake my head no. Even though I love Gramma's soup.

I pull the magic trick book out of my backpack. I sniffle.

"Here, Gramma," I whisper. "I don't need this anymore."

I hand the book to Gramma. She looks confused.

I slink into my room. I drag the not-so-magic cape behind me.

Baby Rabbit hops onto my bed. She holds

my magician's hat in her mouth. She tries to give it to me.

"I don't want it," I sulk. She sticks it in my face again.

"I DON'T WANT IT!" I say louder. I grab it. Then I throw it onto the floor. And stomp, stomp, *stomp* on it.

I pick up my stomped hat. It's squished and wrinkly. I shove it under my bed.

Then I pick up the magic cape.

I throw it in the trash.

Abracadabra-Poof!

I hear Bailey screaming my name through my door. Mom and Daddy must be home.

I whisper, "Abracadabra-poof!"

If I say the extra fancy magic word, maybe I will disappear for real. Then I won't get in trouble for losing Rufus. Or taking Bailey's blankie. I hide under my blanket.

It doesn't work.

"Sit," says Mom. I am already sitting. But I

stay quiet like a mouse. I don't want her to be madder.

"Your teacher called," Daddy says.

"The pet hamster?" Mom interrupts. "Your sister's blanket? *What* were you thinking?"

Bailey storms into my room. She hollers so loud. Her words are jumbled. I do not know a thing she is saying.

Then she starts crying.

I want to cry, too. I sink into my bed. I am as teeny as can be.

Mom and Daddy give me a super-duper long lecture about:

I make my ears very big. I listen.

After they are done lecturing me, Mom takes my animals. She takes Dragon, Tiger, Pink Kitty, Ana, Elsa, Brown Bear, Blue Bear, and Boo-Boo Bear away. She even takes Baby Rabbit.

I do not pout. Or stomp my foot. Or roll on the floor.

Mom says, "When you learn your lesson, you can have them back." She scoots next to me. She rubs my back. Even though it feels very nice, I am still sad.

I sit in my room for a million gazillion hours.

And a million gazillion hours later, I find Mom.

"I learned my lesson," I say to her.

I show her the letter I wrote Ms. Stoltz.

> DEAr Ms. StoLtz,
>
> i Am soRy i mAde RufUs
> DisAppeaR. i am HApee THaT
> we FOWND Him iN the
> cabig patcH. i will
> BE moRE Reesponsibel.
> i PROMise.
>
> LOVE,
>   Bessie

Then I knock on Bailey's door.

"Go away!"

"I'm sorry, Bailey," I say through the door.
Then I leave my most favorite fluffy blanket
outside her door. It is wrapped in a sparkly bow.

"Gah Yee!" Gramma calls from downstairs. I walk to the kitchen very slowly like a sloth.

"Hi, Gramma." I sulk. Gramma's eyes sparkle.

Gramma is sitting at the kitchen table. She pats a chair. Then she puts a little box on the table.

"*Dan tat!*" I say. My favorite! I take a big bite. I *almost* feel all better.

Gramma hands me another box. *What could it be?*

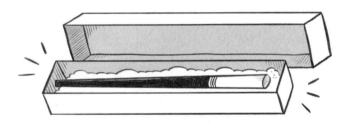

A bamboo stick? Gramma pulls the *Abra-cadabra: Magic for Kids* book from behind her back. She opens to a page with a magic wand.

Gramma points to the bamboo stick. She points to the wand.

My eyes get big. This will be an extra fancy magic wand! I hug Gramma.

"Thank you, Gramma!" I say. "Will you help me?"

Gramma cups my cheeks with both her hands. And gives a little squeeze. We both giggle.

I finish eating my *dan tat*. Then Gramma helps me paint the bamboo stick. We use black paint. And lots of sparkles.

We wait for my wand to dry. I flip through the pages of the magic book with Gramma. She cannot read the words. I can only read a little. But we can both look at the pictures.

I see a page with a magic box. There is a secret bottom. Ooh-la-laddie! I have an extra fancy idea!

Maybe I can still be magical. I remember the lesson I learned from the rice. *Do not let anyone find what you disappeared.*

And the lesson from Rufus. *Always know how you did the trick.*

I still want to make something disappear for the talent show. Just like Houdini! He was a big deal. I will make something disappear, for real. Then I will win the talent show. I make a plan in my head.

Now I just have to practice!

10

Stage Fright

It is finally time for the talent show.

I am next in line to perform. I stand at the bottom of the stage.

"Bessie!" Bailey calls out as she walks up to me. She hands me her blanket. The same one I turned into my magic cape.

"It looks better as a magic cape, anyway," Bailey says. "But, next time, ask first."

"I promise," I say. I squeeze-hug her.

"Okay, okay," she laughs. "Gramma helped

me make it better," says Bailey. "You'll see. Now, get back to the stage. *The show must go on.*"

"Thank you," I say. Bailey walks back to her seat.

Ms. Stoltz gives me a thumbs-up. It is almost time to perform.

My feet feel glued to the floor. And my knees are shaking. I am very nervous.

Margo finishes her performance. She sang a song. And danced, too. Like a real performer! Margo curtsies and everyone claps. She looks right over at me.

Then she walks off the stage. When she struts right by me, her sparkly dress scratches my arm. Margo turns around.

"They're all clapping for me!" says Margo. "Is anyone going to clap for you?"

"Of course!" I say. I stand tall on my tippy-toes.

But I feel teeny. Will *anyone* clap for me?

What if I forget what to do? Then I will not win the talent show. Then I will not perform in the school assembly. I will not be a big deal. I will not be a big anything.

Then I will be too teeny to do anything. *Forever.*

I take a deep breath. Like Mom taught me to.

Ms. Stoltz walks onstage. "Ahem." Ms. Stoltz taps the microphone. "Our next first grader has a very special talent. She is going to perform magic for us. Please welcome Bessie Lee to the stage!" She waves her hand for me to walk onto the stage.

I do not walk.

I stand very still.

I do not blink. I make my body very, very

frozen. Just like a Popsicle.

"You've got this, Bessie!" Bailey calls from the audience.

I look over. She gives me two thumbs-up. I wiggle my fingers. I touch the magic cape. The cape Bailey dug out of the trash can for me.

I let out another slow breath.

"We are ready!" I say. "It won't be like Rufus, Baby Rabbit. You and I *practiced* for a million gazillion days."

I pat Baby Rabbit's shaky paw and hug her. Then we walk onto the stage. "Ahem," I say. I tap the microphone like Ms. Stoltz did.

"I am *Teeny* Houdini," I say. "Just like Harry Houdini. The greatest magician of all time. Except I am not Harry. I am Bessie. And I am teeny. So I am Teeny Houdini. And I will be a great magician, too!"

I hold up the name tag I made. It has "Teeny Houdini" written on it. It's extra big with swirly letters.

"This is my assistant, Baby Rabbit," I say. Baby Rabbit hides under my cape.

"Come say hi, Baby Rabbit," I try again.

I hold her up so everyone can see her.

Baby Rabbit quivers. She is scared. I rub her head. I put her down on the table next to me. "We can do this," I whisper.

Baby Rabbit looks calmer. I turn to the audience. "Are you ready for magic?" I ask. I use my loud, outside voice.

"Yes!" shouts the crowd.

"Okay!" I say. "First, I need a magical wand.

I will pull it out of this little envelope," I say. I stick out my elbow. My left hand and the envelope hide the wand. Just like Bailey and I practiced.

"One, two, three. Abracadabra-poof!" I say. Just like a real magician.

I pull a long, black wand out of the envelope.

"Ooh!" says Ella. She watches from the bottom of the stage.

The audience cheers. I wiggle my cape. The shimmery ribbons make sparkles when the stage lights shine on them. Just like a real performer.

"Now I will perform my big magic trick," I say. "I will make my assistant, Baby Rabbit, disappear," I say loudly.

"Sure you will," says Margo from the crowd. She rolls her eyes.

I do not pay attention to her.

I show the audience my big, empty black box.

"Ready, Baby Rabbit?" I ask.

Baby Rabbit shakes her head.

What?!

Then Baby Rabbit darts off the stage.

11

The Grand Disappearing Act!

*O*h *no.* I am on the stage by myself. My magic trick is to make Baby Rabbit disappear in the big black box. But Baby Rabbit ran off the stage. How can I do my magic trick without her? How can I win the talent show without her?

"One moment, please," I say to the audience.

This is not *what we practiced.*

I walk to the side of the stage. I peek behind the curtain.

"Baby Rabbit?"

Baby Rabbit's ears flop over her eyes. She is shaking.

Oh no. This is not what we practiced at all.

"It's okay, Baby Rabbit." I hug her tight. Then I kiss her head.

The show must go on. Just like Bailey said. Just like Harry Houdini would say. Real magicians keep going. They improvise. *Improvise* means you keep going. And you change when something is not what you practiced.

Like when your very best buddy, Baby Rabbit, is too scared to disappear in the box. And you love her. So you will disappear for her, instead.

Even though you've never done it before.

I will keep going. I will disappear in the box. *The show must go on.*

I walk over to Ms. Stoltz. I whisper into her ear. Then I look out at Bailey in the audience. I wave her over. When she comes over, I whisper in her ear, too.

"Are you sure?" whispers Bailey.

I nod.

I walk back into the spotlight.

"Now I will perform my big magic trick," I say.

"How?" Margo calls out.

"I will make *myself* disappear," I say to the audience.

Everyone gasps.

"First, I will make the box magic. Then I will go inside. My new assistant, Bailey, will close the lid. And then I will disappear."

I zoom the box from one side of the stage to the other.

"See how the box is empty?" I ask.

The crowd nods. Everyone is paying very close attention.

"One, two, three." I tap the box with my magical wand. I wave my magical cape. Glitter flies out of the pockets that Gramma helped Bailey sew together.

"Now the box is magic," I say. "I will turn the box on its side. Now I will get in," I say.

I carefully crawl inside. Bailey winks at me.

"I will give my assistant my magic wand. She will close the lid and say the magic words. Then I will disappear. Ready?" I ask. I am sitting in the box.

"YES!" roars the crowd.

Bailey closes the lid. She taps the wand on the box.

She says, "Abracadabra-poof!"

Bailey opens the box. It looks empty! She turns the box toward the corner of the stage. Just like I asked her to. Now my class can see.

"WOW!!!" says Chris.

"Way cool!" says Ella. Gorkem and Brayden nod and clap. Margo stares in shock.

I can see Margo's face. I peek out from a teeny cutout hole in the box.

I whisper-giggle. I am squished in the secret bottom of the box. The box is big for a rabbit. But small for a person. Good thing I am teeny. Or else I would not fit in the box. Then this trick would never work!

I feel the cheesy doodles that I put in here for Baby Rabbit. I chomp, chomp, chomp. The audience claps. They think I disappeared for real. They do not know that I am in the secret bottom of the box.

"Ready for Teeny Houdini to reappear?" Bailey asks the crowd.

Bailey throws my magic cape over the box. She waves my magical wand and taps the box.

She pulls the cape away. Then I jump out of the box super-duper fast.

Glitter flies all around.

"TA-DA! I'M BACK," I yell.

The crowd cheers.

"Thanks!" I whisper to Bailey. She runs off the stage.

I strut to the front of the stage like a mighty magician. Then I twirl my cape around me.

I walk right up to the edge. I tip my hat.

And take a large bow. Everyone claps loudly.

I am a big deal!

Even though I am teeny. Teeny enough to fit in the secret bottom of the box. Teeny enough to *wow* the crowd.

I am teeny. And I am a great magician.

Just like Houdini.

I am Teeny Houdini!